0 0001 6389885 1

TRAILS WEST
9-10-01

W9-CAO-803

TRICK-
or-
TREAT
on
MILTON
STREET

TRICK-or-TREAT ON MILTON STREET

BY

LISA BULLARD

ILLUSTRATED BY

JONI OELTJENBRUNS

CAROLRHODA BOOKS, INC./MINNEAPOLIS

Text copyright © 2001 by Lisa Bullard
Illustrations copyright © 2001 by Joni Oeltjenbruns

All rights reserved. International copyright secured. No
part of this book may be reproduced, stored in a retrieval
system, or transmitted in any form or by any means—
electronic, mechanical, photocopying, recording, or
otherwise—without the prior written permission of
Carolrhoda Books, Inc., except for the inclusion of brief
quotations in an acknowledged review.

Carolrhoda Books, Inc.
A division of Lerner Publishing Group
241 First Avenue North
Minneapolis, MN 55401 U.S.A.

Website address: www.lernerbooks.com

Library of Congress Cataloging-in-Publication Data

Bullard, Lisa.
   Trick-or-treat on Milton Street / by Lisa Bullard;
illustrations by Joni Oeltjenbruns.
      p.   cm.
   Summary: Charley is sure that the first Halloween in his
new house will be awful, until his stepfather takes him
out trick-or-treating.
   ISBN: 1-57505-158-3 (lib. bdg. : alk. paper)
   [I. Halloween—Fiction.] I. Oeltjenbruns, Joni, ill.
II. Title.
PZ7.B91245 Tr 2001
[E]—dc21   00-010750

Manufactured in the United States of America
1 2 3 4 5 6 - JR- 06 05 04 03 02 01

For Mom, who taught me that
words taste as good as candy;
and for Dad, who called me
"Punkin": Trick or Treat!
L.B.

To my favorite goblins:
Mikaela, Devan, Kade, Dayna,
Matalin, Erin, Bridget, Shane,
Riley, Derek, Reid, Chase, Corbin,
Maren, Caleb, Carli, Gabriele,
Macey, Maiah, Elijah, Becky,
Vicky, Matt, and Heather!
J.O.

Charley's mom looked really bad. In fact, she looked frightful. "Ohh," she groaned, "I'm sick." "Sick?" said Charley. "It's Halloween! You can't be sick!"

Charley was living in a strange new town in a strange new house on boring old Milton Street, where he didn't have one single friend. How was he supposed to make friends when there was nobody around but grown-ups?

"You're supposed to take me trick-or-treating!" Charley wailed.

"Don't worry, Charley," mumbled Mom around the thermometer in her mouth. "Dave can take you."

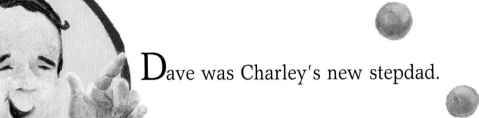

Dave was Charley's new stepdad.

He was always doing
something to embarrass
Charley. Like when he
juggled too many
oranges at the grocery
store and dropped them
all over the floor.

Or when he tried to do a magic trick at a restaurant and knocked everything off their table.

"Hey, champ," said Dave, "I know Milton Street better than anybody. I grew up here. It's the best place to trick-or-treat that you've ever—"

"Maybe I'll just skip Halloween this year," interrupted Charley. And he ran upstairs to his room.

Charley lay on top of his new bunk bed and kicked his toe at the ceiling. Now he had no friends and no Mom to trick-or-treat with, just Dave and a neighborhood full of old people. What did grown-ups do on Halloween when there weren't any kids around?

They'd probably decide "dressing up" for Halloween should mean wearing suits and ties instead of real costumes.

They'd think that pumpkins were too messy, and carve faces in something tidier, like green peppers. Grown-ups would want to go trick-or-treating in the middle of the day, so that nobody missed their bedtime. Instead of candy bars and gum, they'd want stuff that was good for you—like carrots and brussels sprouts and broccoli.

And how could old people bob for apples? Wouldn't their false teeth fall out?

Charley had nearly given up
on Halloween altogether when
he heard Dave call, "Charley,
it's getting late! Last chance to
trick-or-treat on Milton Street!"

Charley slowly trudged downstairs. Dave was waiting by the front door. He was all bundled up for a chilly autumn night, and he was wearing the GOOFIEST-looking hat Charley had ever seen.

"Let's go, champ," said Dave. Charley didn't want to go anywhere with that hat. He almost turned around and went right back up the stairs.

But before he knew it, Mom had pushed him out the door.

Charley stepped
outside and looked
around. Even he had
to admit that boring
old Milton Street
didn't look too bad.

Dave nudged Charley toward a cobweb-draped house with a black cat in the front window. A green-skinned, warty-nosed, scary old witch opened the door.

"Um, trick or treat?" Charley said.

"Come in, dearie," cackled the witch. "You're just the kind of tasty imp my witch's brew could use."

"I'm not an imp," said Charley, inching closer to Dave. "I'm an alien."

"An alien—excellent! Just look what I have for you," said the witch. She was starting to sound an awful lot like Mrs. Brumflier, a lady who worked in the school cafeteria. She handed Charley a huge caramel apple.

At the next house, they were greeted by a chubby mummy trailing bandages from head to toe. A skeleton waggled a long, knobby finger at Charley.

"Marcus and Rita, this is my stepson, Charley," Dave said proudly.

"Do all the grown-ups dress up around here?" asked Charley.

"We're going to a costume party later," the skeleton explained.

The mummy held out a bowl full of candy bars.
"Take two—you don't want to end up looking like that,"
he whispered, pointing at the skeleton's bony ribs.

Charley looked up at the dark house on the corner. "I don't think anyone's home," he said. Then the door creaked slowly open.

At first they could see nothing but flickering candlelight.

Then a vampire appeared out of nowhere. The sharp points of his shiny white teeth glistened.

"Anybody thirsty?" asked the vampire. "I've got some delicious red punch I've made for the party I'm attending this evening. Or would you rather pay a visit to the bats in my attic?"

The vampire handed Charley a glow-in-the-dark toothbrush. "Here's a little something to make your teeth as strong and white as mine," he said.

"Dr. Phang is my dentist," whispered Dave.

At each house on Milton Street, the door opened on a big surprise. There was a cowgirl with gray hair, glasses, and a horse that barked.

Frankenstein's monster danced with the biggest ballerina Charley had ever seen.

There was a pirate who kept stepping on his beard, and a pink-and-green striped ghost.

Charley's jack-o'-lantern bag filled up quickly, and before he knew it, he found himself back in front of his own house.

"I guess we should go see how Mom's feeling," he said.

"I'll bet she's doing better," said Dave.

As they started up the walk, the front door of their house flew open.

"Surprise!" yelled Mom.
She looked even worse than
before. Her head was wrapped
in bandages, her arm was in a
sling, and she was wearing a
hospital gown.

Then Charley realized that
behind her were a witch and a
skeleton and a mummy . . . all
the people he had met that night.

"WELCOME TO MILTON
STREET, CHARLEY!" they cheered.

It was a great party. Dr. Phang's vampire punch was delicious. Mrs. Brumflier had brought her witch's brew, which to Charley's relief tasted like chili. Everybody danced the bunny hop and then told spooky ghost stories. Dave juggled four popcorn balls, and he didn't drop a single one!

And when they bobbed for apples, the only teeth that fell out were Dr. Phang's fangs.

As he waved good-bye to his new friends at the end of the night, Charley noticed something. "Hey, Dave," he said. "Everybody else dressed up for Halloween. Why didn't you wear a costume?"

"I did, Charley," said Dave. "Didn't you notice my hat?" Charley nodded.

"It's the same hat my dad wore back when he took me out to trick-or-treat on Milton Street. I thought the best costume I could wear tonight was to dress up like a dad."

Charley looked at Dave. Then he looked at the hat. "You know," said Charley, "I think I'm going to like living

Our First Halloween on Milton Street